The Trickster Ghost

The Trickster Ghost

by Ellen Showell

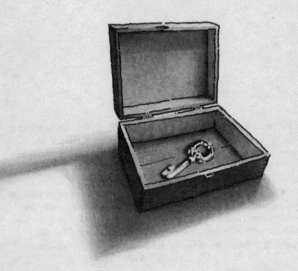

Illustrated by Karen A. Jerome

SCHOLASTIC INC.
NEW YORK TORONTO LONDON AUCKLAND SYDNEY

No part of this publication may be reproduced in whole or in part, or stored in a retrieval system, or transmitted in any form or by any means, electronic, mechanical, photocopying, recording, or otherwise, without written permission of the publisher. For information regarding permission, write to Scholastic Inc., 730 Broadway, New York, NY 10003.

ISBN 0-590-45795-0

12 11 10 9 8 7 6 5 4 3   2 3 4 5 6 7/9

Printed in the U.S.A.   28

First Scholastic printing, October 1992

*To Rachael and Stephen,
who wanted a ghost story*

Contents

The Trickster Ghost

Chapter One

It's Not Fair!

"**I** didn't take your dumb elephant!" said Stephen Goodman.

"Well, she's gone, and somebody took her." Rachael was standing so close, he couldn't make the porch swing move without hitting her. She wasn't shouting. She was ten and very different from eight-year-old Stephen. Her voice stayed calm and even. "Stevie, I have a lot of stuffed animals, but only one Calico. When we moved here, she was the first thing I unpacked. I put her on my new bed so it would seem like home."

"I didn't take her!" Stephen let the swing

1

go right into her knees. "Just because I hid your skates, and that was a long time ago, I don't take things now!"

She jumped back, gave him a long look, and went into the house.

Stephen's body was tense with anger. To calm down, he stayed on the swing and let it slow gradually. The squeak of the chains was a song in his head, "Not me! Not me! Not me! Not me!"

Calico was the fourth thing to disappear since they had moved into the big old house in West Lawrence, Kansas. Everyone blamed Stephen.

He rubbed his palm against the ragged edge of a broken board. The wood was so old and soft. It smelled like roses. He liked almost everything about Grandma and Grandpa's house, which was now his house.

Stephen and his family had moved into the house right after Grandpa and Grandma

Percy moved out. Grandpa had an ailing heart. He could no longer do the kind of hard work a big house and yard requires. It was too much for Grandma, too. So the old people had moved to a nearby apartment and let their daughter and her family have the house.

Almost everything needed fixing. Dad spent every Saturday working on the roof or building new porch steps or painting. The house had been built over an even older house, a log cabin. In some places they could see the original logs.

Mother was slowly changing the house to suit her. But it still looked a lot the way Stephen remembered from visits. In the front hall, roses still climbed up the walls — on wallpaper, of course. And there was the silly closet that didn't have a door. A blue-and-white-striped curtain hung over it to hide the coats and boots.

The first thing to disappear after they

moved in was one of Stephen's rocks — his best one. It was rough and almost round, big as a man's fist. He could see shiny pieces of mica in it. It brought him luck. Was anybody upset about that being gone? No! It was, "Oh, you just lost it in the moving, Stevie. You'll find another rock just as nice as that one."

Well, a week later, Grandma's hourglass wasn't on the kitchen windowsill, where it was supposed to be, and no one could find it. Stephen knew exactly what it looked like. It was about six inches tall and squeezed in the middle and had sand in it. When all the sand ran from the top to the bottom, three minutes were up. Grandma said she didn't take it with her because she knew her daughter had loved it ever since she was little.

"Have you been playing with the hourglass, Stephen?" his mother had asked when she found it missing.

"I was looking at it, but I put it back," Stephen had told her.

"Now who would take the hourglass?" Mother had asked.

"Well, who took my rock?" Stephen had said. And that's when they began suspecting him. They seemed to think he was somehow getting even, trying to make them care.

Soon after that, Ardis, who was Rachael and Stephen's thirteen-year-old sister, had stomped into the computer room where they were playing a game. "The seashell Mark Wiley brought me from California is gone from my dresser where I put it!" she'd raged. "Somebody around here snoops into other people's rooms and helps himself to whatever he likes!"

"Don't look at me!" Stephen had replied.

"Don't blame Stephen!" Rachael had said. She usually took up for him.

Now Calico, Rachael's elephant, was missing, and even Rachael blamed Stephen. He wanted to kick or punch something. He started the swing up again and made it go as high as he could. He didn't care if it broke.

He was still swinging when Grandma and Grandpa arrived for their weekly visit.

Chapter Two

No One Will Believe

Stephen was so mad at the way they were treating him that he thought about not going to dinner that night. But he didn't want to hurt Grandpa and Grandma's feelings. He wasn't hungry and he didn't speak at the table. Why should he? They thought he was a thief and a liar. He ate one required pea.

The others were talking about the changes the Goodmans were making in the house. "You all do what you want," Grandma said. "It's your house now."

Grandpa said, "What about the closet door?"

"That's up to my daughter," she answered. "It's only because of her I kept it like that. She made me take that door off many years ago. Now she can put it back or leave it off, whatever she wants."

They all looked at Mrs. Goodman. "Why did you want it off, Mom?" asked Stephen, forgetting he wasn't speaking.

"Yes, honey, why?" asked Mr. Goodman. "I thought I'd get to that chore next week, put in a real door there."

"Oh, I don't know why," she said. "I just want it the way it is, with the curtain. There are enough other things to work on." She got up from the table and started cleaning the kitchen.

"Well!" said Grandpa. "What's this I hear about things disappearing?"

Stephen said, "May I be excused?"

Later, he found Rachael working on a poster on the living room floor. He squatted near her. "Rachael, I'm really not the one taking things," he said.

She kept painting. He watched her sideways. He could get a better idea of what she was thinking that way. He waited for a smile to steal over her face, and for her to say, "Stevie, I believe you." But all she said was, "So who is it? It's not me. I seriously doubt if it's Ardis or Mom or Dad."

"I don't know, Rachael," Stephen answered. "But it's not me, either. There has to be someone else in this house."

"An invisible stranger." He could tell she believed no such thing.

He went to bed and lay there trying to think. Rachael came in and sat beside him. She said softly, "Stevie, please don't keep this up. I'll tell you what I think could be the truth. Your rock got lost when we moved. Things always do. Then, you were playing with the hourglass and dropped it and maybe it broke. Maybe you were afraid to tell Mom, so you picked up the pieces and hid them."

Stephen said, "And what did I do with the sand?"

"You could have swept it up. And then you had to keep the stories going about things disappearing, so you also hid the other things. Well, Stephen, you know how I feel about Calico. Just bring back my elephant and Ardis's shell, and I will get a new hourglass for Mom, and no one will say any more about it."

Stephen turned away from her and curled up on the bed. What was the use?

She touched his hair. "Please, Stevie."

He sat up and looked Rachael right in the eye. "Rachael, I didn't. And, somehow, I'll prove it to you." He pulled the covers over his head.

Chapter Three

Nothing for Little Boys?

When Stephen finally went to sleep, he dreamed. In his dream, his rock, the hourglass, the shell, and Calico were all found in his dresser drawer. It was so real, he even got up to go look. Nothing but his clothes were there. He got back in bed and tried to stay awake and listen for someone sneaking around. He whispered, "Whoever you are . . .

. . . I'm going to catch you," he said when he awoke the next morning. As he got dressed, he was quiet and watchful. Before raising the window shade, he peeked out at the yard. Just the usual quiet of a Sunday morning. He began searching the upstairs for places someone might hide. He saw no sign of anyone. He walked downstairs to the landing that was halfway down, where the stairs made a turn. On the landing was a high-backed bench that was more than a bench. Under its seat was a hollow place for storing things. He lifted the seat and looked inside. It was full of blankets.

Next, he wanted to look in the attic, but it was too spooky. He needed an excuse to get someone to go with him.

"Ardis!" he called. "Will you help me find something in the attic? That's where Mom put our box of old records. I want to get one out and play it."

She followed him up the narrow stairs to the big, dimly lighted room under the eaves. The attic was full of old lamps, broken chairs, piles of magazines — things Grandma and Grandpa had left. Ardis said,

"Stevie, did you hide the missing things up here and now want me to find them?"

"No!" he said. "Go ahead and look for them. But whatever you find, remember it wasn't me who put them there."

Ardis found the box of records right away. Then she and Stephen searched for the missing things. Stephen was looking in the shadows and corners for a place someone might hide. But there was no sign of anyone.

A ragged old quilt was thrown over something in a dark corner. Stephen pulled it off to reveal a large, musty-smelling trunk.

"What's in this?" he asked Ardis.

"That's Grandma's trunk. It has a lot of things she's keeping — fancy gowns she wore when she was young, baby shoes, old letters, and pictures and stuff from her family."

"I've never gotten to see inside it," said Stephen.

"There's nothing of interest to little boys."

"Humph!" grunted Stephen. He tried to lift the trunk's high, rounded lid, but it was locked.

"Stephen, I don't think you or anybody else opened up that trunk to hide stuff," said Ardis. "I doubt if Mom even knows where the key is. It hasn't been opened for years."

Back in his room, Stephen looked through the box of records. He found one he had liked when he was little, and put it on his record player. He was disgusted when nothing sounded but scratches and then, over and over because the record was stuck:

". . . many long years, many long years, many long years, many long years, many long years, many long years . . ."

"Ago," said Rachael, who was standing

in the doorway. "The old grey mare she ain't what she used to be, many long years ago."

"I know," said Stephen, turning off the record.

"Mother wants you," she said.

Chapter Four

Caught!

Mrs. Goodman said, "Stephen, honey, you are at an age when it's hard sometimes to know the difference between what is real and what is just a story. Sometimes we do things and wish we hadn't, and so we say we didn't do them and almost believe it."

"Mother, it's not me taking things. There is someone we don't know about in this house!" said Stephen.

Mrs. Goodman stood up angrily. "Stephen! I will have no more talk about any 'someone else.' Do you hear?"

Stephen ran downstairs and ducked past

the curtain into the front hall closet. He slid down against the wall. He heard his mother running down the stairs. The front door opened. She was calling, "Stephen? Where are you? Frank, Rachael, help me find Stephen!" He heard them go out.

Let Mom and Dad and all of them look for him. He would stay in the closet forever. He closed his eyes. The house was quiet. Stephen felt like he was dissolving. The house was taking him, like it took the other things. He didn't care. It smelled nice in the closet. It smelled of roses and long ago.

He didn't know how long he was there before the noise came.

pi dit. pit dit. pi dit.

dit dit dit dit dit dit dit

dit

dit

dit

dit

dit dit dit

He recognized the sound. Marbles. Something lightly touched his leg. He could feel it, so he knew he was still a flesh-and-blood boy. He opened his eyes and pulled back the curtain. His big blue-and-yellow marble that should have been in a bag under his bed lay against him. More marbles were dropping down the steps.

"Hello?" he called upstairs. "Rachael? Ardis? Anybody?"

One last marble, a little red one, rolled to a halt and was still.

Stephen tiptoed up the stairs. On the landing were all of his white marbles. They were arranged in a circle on the rug, next to the high-backed bench. He was picking them up when he heard a slight creak and turned around. The lid to the bench was up. A blanket was hanging over the edge as though someone had pulled it halfway out.

"I'll get blamed for this," Stephen muttered to himself. He was tucking the blanket back down into the storage place when the rug slid out from under his feet and he tumbled inside.

The lid slammed down.

Chapter Five

Rachael Believes

Stephen tried to push up the lid of the bench, but it wouldn't budge. "Hey!" he shouted. There was a noise like the heels of somebody's shoes kicking the outside of the chest. "LET ME OUT OF HERE!" he hollered.

The racket kept up. "CUT IT OUT!" he yelled. Stephen burrowed down among the blankets and covered his ears.

A door banged and feet clattered on the stairs.

"STEVIE!" It was Rachael's voice. "Stevie, where are you?"

"Let me out, Rachael!"

The lid opened, and Rachael peered down at him. "Stevie, what are you doing in there?"

"Rachael, that wasn't funny!" He was beating on her with his fists and could hardly keep from crying. "You shouldn't have done that, Rachael!"

She held his arms. "Stevie, I just got here. I wasn't doing anything! You look scared to death!"

"Yes you were here! You threw down those marbles and you sat on the bench and wouldn't let me out! It was you all the time, wasn't it, Rachael? You were playing tricks. Well, I'll never believe another word you say."

"Stevie, I promise, it wasn't me. I just came in. Mom and Dad are looking for you, and I was, too, until I got to thinking. I had an idea you might be hiding in the house."

"Hah!" said Stevie. "You were here all along."

"Please, Stevie. Believe me."

"Why should I? You never believe me anymore."

"I do now. Nobody could fake looking so scared. Were you hurt?"

"No. But the kicking made me mad. It was giving me a headache. And it's no fun feeling like you're shut up in a box. It's not the best breathing down there."

"It wasn't me, Stevie."

"Yes it was. And I bet you were the one taking things, letting people think it was me."

"You don't really think that."

"Well, you really thought I did it."

"Stevie, it's just that . . . what's the matter?"

Stevie could only point. Rachael turned around and saw her jump rope turning round and round in the air, as though someone were skipping. Except no one was visible.

"I believe you, Rachael," whispered Stephen.

"And I believe you, Stevie!"

Mrs. Goodman had come into the house and was calling, "Rachael? Did you find him?"

The rope dropped to the landing floor and lay still.

"Stephen!" said his mother. "What on earth have you been doing? Do you realize we have been looking all over the neighborhood for you?"

"Mother, Stephen's right, there's someone else in this house. Someone we can't see!"

"Rachael!" shouted Mrs. Goodman. "Not you, too!"

Mr. Goodman came in. "Son, didn't you hear us calling you?" he said.

"Nobody would believe me, Dad. I wanted to be alone. But I wasn't alone. There's somebody . . ."

"Now, Stephen!" Mrs. Goodman warned.

Her husband said, "Honey, it's an old

house, and the kids have heard stories about haunted houses. You know what imaginations they have. I'll talk to Stephen later.

"Right now, you guys get these marbles picked up," he went on.

"Not me," mumbled Stephen when they had gone. "I didn't put them down, so I don't have to pick them up."

Rachael said, "Stevie, then I'll have to do it, and I didn't put them down, either. You help, and then we'll figure out . . . what to do."

Chapter Six

Getting Close

"I guess they're all clues," said Rachael.

"What all?" asked Stephen. They were sitting on the porch swing, their best thinking place.

"The missing things. They are clues to who took them and to how a rope can turn by itself."

While the swing creaked, they said the names of the things over and over. A rock. An elephant. An hourglass. A shell. A rock. An elephant. An hourglass. A shell.

"What do we know about elephants?" asked Rachael finally.

"They live a long time, and have long

memories, and have trunks," said Stephen.

"And your rock?" asked Rachael.

"Well, it's hard. Rocks last a long time. And mine is more than just a rock. It's got shiny bits of mica in it. And it brings me luck, or used to."

"It is a very mysterious rock if it does that," said Rachael.

"Yeah. You can't see that part of it. You just have to believe it."

"What about an hourglass?" said Rachael.

"It's about time," said Stephen.

"What?"

"I mean, when the sand runs through, the time is up. Like if you're cooking an egg. It's done."

"Oh. Then what about the shell?"

Stephen sighed. She was making him do all the thinking. "I don't know. Something in a shell is hidden. I mean, you can't see what's on the inside."

"It has sand in it, too," said Rachael.

"Ardis says she can hear the sea in it. It's like a voice from far away and long ago."

"I have an idea of something else the things might mean," said Stephen. "Give me a pencil and paper."

"You've got a pencil," Rachael said. "It's in your shirt pocket."

"Huh? Oh. How did that get there?"

"I don't know. Look, a sheet of paper just blew up on the porch. What are you going to write?"

"You'll see." Stephen wrote the name of each missing thing.

"Hey, I'm right! Look, Rachael. Look at the first letter of each word. R for rock, O for ourglass, S for shell, and E for elephant. It spells Rose! That's a clue!"

"Stevie, I hate to tell you this, but 'hourglass' is spelled with an 'h.' You made the mistake because the 'h' is silent. RHSE doesn't spell anything."

Stephen was red-faced.

"Any more bright ideas?" she asked.

"Your turn."

"I think it's a child," said Rachael. "He or she plays. Like with your marbles and my jump rope."

"Listen!"

Someone was singing "The Old Grey Mare."

"That's not Ardis," said Rachael. "Or Mom."

"It's sure not Dad," said Stephen.

It was a child's voice. It came from above them. They ran upstairs.

Chapter Seven

A Plea

"It's coming from the attic," said Rachael when they reached the upstairs hallway.

They carefully opened the door to the stairs and went up as noiselessly as possible.

"It's coming from over there," whispered Stephen when they were under the eaves. He. pointed to the trunk in the corner. The singing kept up softly.

Ain't what she used to be, ain't what she used to be . . .

They reached for each other's hands. Together they stepped around boxes and furniture until they were at the trunk. It was

quiet. Rachael put her head against the lid. She shrank back. "Listen!"

Stephen put his ear down.

"Open."

A voice came from inside.

"We can't," said Stephen in a shaking voice. The plea came again.

"Open."

Stephen was dizzy. He held on to Rachael and she to him. They backed away. Downstairs, Stephen said, "What do you think it was, Rachael?"

"Someone wants us to open the trunk."

"Do you think we should?"

"Do you?" she asked.

Stephen was scared. But he was also curious. He would never feel right if they didn't open the trunk, somehow.

"Mom sure won't try to find the key if we say anything about ghosts," said Rachael.

"Ghosts?"

"Isn't that what we are hearing and

seeing, or not seeing?" asked Rachael. "Your 'someone else' is a ghost, and a little one, who wants the trunk open."

"We could say we want to see the gold and silver," said Stephen. "Or the sword."

"It's not a pirate's chest."

Ardis came out on the porch. "What are you two plotting?" she asked.

"Ardis," said Rachael, "do you think Dad would show Stephen what's in the old trunk up in the attic? He's got all these ideas about it being full of swords and goblins. . . ."

"I never said goblins."

"It's giving him nightmares," said Rachael. "You had a bad dream last night, didn't you, Stephen?"

"Yes," Stephen said.

"So if he could see what's really in it, he could get it off his mind."

Ardis agreed to talk to their grandmother, who said to look for the key in a wooden box on a shelf in the basement. "But she said open the trunk only if Mom wanted to," Ardis reported.

At first, Mrs. Goodman said no. "We have so many of our own things to get in order now, it's not the time to go looking into things that have been put away for years," she said.

But their dad thought it was time to open it up. "There might be things in it that should be aired out," he said.

The key had lain inside the box for so long that when he picked it up, it left a key-shaped outline on the bottom.

They all trooped up to the attic.

Chapter Eight

The Opening

"Turn the key hard, Dad," urged Stephen.

"Hurry!" said Rachael.

"Let me try," said Ardis. She knelt down and blew inside the lock. She polished the key with the tail of her blouse.

"Come on, Ardis!" said Stephen.

She carefully inserted the key into the lock and turned. "I've got it."

Everyone pulled on the lid until it sprang up. They fell backwards in a whirly blur of whiteness. Feathers filled the air and flew in their eyes, noses, and hair.

"How in the world did that get untied?" Mrs. Goodman brushed feathers from her face and hair. "It was feathers from an old mattress tick that somebody was supposed to make pillows out of someday. I helped mother tie it up myself twenty years ago!"

Stephen and Rachael looked at each other — and around the room. Stephen asked his mother, "What else is in there?"

"Lots of things." She pulled out a white organdy dress and shook it. Stephen's eyes widened as he saw what she found next. It was a yellow-and-blue creature with floppy ears and a long trunk. He grinned. "Mom, do you remember an elephant being in here?"

Rachael screamed, "It's Calico!"

Stephen plunged his hand into the trunk and felt among satin slippers, letters, and bags full of baby booties until he found his missing rock and the hourglass. He held them up triumphantly. Ardis plunged in and came up with an object that had been carefully wrapped in a linen handkerchief edged with torn lace. "It's my shell!" she said. She held it to her ear. "I can still hear the sea."

"This is impossible!" said Mrs. Goodman. "No one could have opened this trunk without the key!"

"Here is a sword!" said Stephen gleefully. "I knew it!" He pulled out a long silver blade from under a box that had been tied with string. The string was cut.

"That sword belonged to my uncle," said his mother. "He had it when he was in military school. How did it get out of its sheath?"

"All this is very, very strange," said Mr. Goodman.

Rachael looked in the box. "Mom, there are pictures. Do you know any of these people?"

"Let me see," said her mother. "No. Your grandmother probably . . . oh." She stopped

as she came to a small picture near the bottom. Her face was white.

"What is it, Mom?" asked Ardis.

Stephen peeked. She was holding a picture of a little girl with long dark pigtails, sitting on a porch swing.

"Who is she, Mom?" asked Rachael.

Mrs. Goodman swallowed as though trying to keep back a memory. "She was someone I used to play with when I was little."

"What was her name, Mom?" asked Stephen.

Mrs. Goodman looked at her husband. "I've never told anyone about what happened," she said. "I thought I had pushed it out of my memory. But now that I see her picture, I know she's always been there, in my mind."

"What is it you're trying to tell us, honey?" asked her husband.

Mrs. Goodman said sadly, "Her name was Rose."

Chapter Nine

A Day in the Past

"When I was seven years old, I heard someone singing outside on the porch, and I went out to see who it was."

Mrs. Goodman was telling her story.

"A little girl was on the swing, making it go as high as she could. 'Stop!' I told her, and she did. 'Who are you?' I asked.

"She said, 'My name is Rose. Are you seven?'

" 'Yes,' I said.

" 'I am, too,' she said. 'I want someone to play with.'

" 'Where do you live?' I asked.

" 'In my house,' she answered. But she wouldn't say where that was. I was glad for a friend. We played paper dolls that day, and mother brought us cookies. Rose came back often. She always wore the same faded cotton dress and always went home about four o'clock.' "

"Did you find out where she lived?" asked Stephen.

"She wouldn't say. She smiled or laughed when I asked."

"I would have followed her home to see," said Stephen.

"I tried. She just stayed still until I went indoors. But one day she made me mad. She kept singing loudly in my ear when I was talking on the telephone to another friend. So I said, 'Rose, there's a surprise for you in the hall closet.'

"When she went in, I shut the door and wouldn't open it. It had a real wooden door then. She kicked and yelled for a long time.

At four o'clock, she hushed. When I opened the door, she was gone. I never saw her again."

"How did she get out?" asked Ardis.

"I never knew," said Mrs. Goodman. "I was right there beside the door for the whole time. No one came out."

"She became invisible," said Stephen. "She could do that because she was a ghost. And she still is. She goes with this house."

Rachael said, "Rose must be the one who took things and somehow got them into the trunk. She's probably been a ghost so long, she's learned how to do spooky tricks."

Stephen said, "She might have lived in this house when it was just a little old log cabin. She probably died young, and part of her stays here."

"You mean this house is haunted?" asked Ardis, looking around her.

"Yes," said Rachael. "It's like there is

a wall between her own time and now. She finds holes in it."

They all looked over their shoulders. The only things ghostly they saw were feathers floating in the air.

Chapter Ten

Remembered

After dinner that night, Rachael and Stephen took their photograph album out on the porch swing. They put Rose's picture right between their own. "I think this is what she wanted," said Stephen. "Not to be forgotten."

He wrote her name under the picture.

R O S E

"You were right about her name, after all," said Rachael. "I guess she spelled 'hourglass' the same way you did, with an O at the beginning."

"Of course," said Stephen. "It's sensible."

Their father came out carrying a hammer

49

and nails. "You two will have to move," he said.

"Why?" they asked.

"I'm going to fix the hole in the back of that swing."

"No, Dad, please," said Stephen. "Leave it."

"Stevie!" said Rachael. "Do you think that was the way Rose came?"

He shrugged. "There are lots of holes. It had to be a certain kind of hole. An old, friendly hole."

So Mr. Goodman did as Stephen wished and let the broken place be.

Just in case Rose was still on *their* side of time, Stephen and Rachael sat apart on the swing, to leave space in the middle.

There were no more tricks in the house. But, often, in the morning, they would look out and see the swing sailing high.

When it slowed down, and the chains creaked, to Stephen they sang this song:

Many long years ago, many long years ago, many long years ago . . .

About the Author

Ellen Showell grew up near Lewisberg, West Virginia, in the Greenbrier Valley. There were four children in her family. She graduated from Berea College, in Berea, Kentucky, majoring in English. After college she did some adventurous traveling, including spending time on an Indian reservation.

Ms. Showell chose to settle in the Washington, D.C., area, where she began her writing career. At first, she wrote for advertising and public relations firms. Later, she wrote for the government's Economic Opportunity Program of the 1960s and 70s. She began writing for children when her own son was twelve.

Ellen Showell is known as Penny to her friends. She lives in Arlington, Virginia, with her husband, John Showell.